MY CHINATOWN

ONE YEAR IN POEMS BY KAM MAK

HARPERCOLLINSPUBLISHERS

Back home in Hong Kong,
it's New Year.
Papa says we'll have New Year here,
in America, in Chinatown.
Mama says it will be just like home.

But it isn't home,
even when the firecrackers
hiss and crackle all night long
to scare off every evil spirit in the world.
In the morning, I go out alone
to kick through drifts of red paper.
Somewhere there will be one whole firecracker
hidden, waiting for me.

But I can't find one,
even though the air dances
with scraps of red,
a snowfall the color of luck.
It must be someone else's luck this year.
Not mine.

WINTER

In Hong Kong, my grandmother
is in her kitchen
making pickled kumquats.

In Chinatown, there are kumquats
piled high on every street cart,
wooden crates packed full of suns.
Mama takes forever, hunting for
the ones with leaves attached.
Leaves are good luck.

But she doesn't know how to pickle them.
Grandmother wouldn't tell her.
"If I told you, you'd never come to see me again!"
she said, and winked,
slipping one last kumquat
into my bowl.

The fortune-teller sits outside,
huddled on her stool,
buried in her coat,
hat down over her forehead.

Mama tells her all about me—
my name, when I was born
(the Year of the Ox, in the afternoon).
But she never brings me along.

Instead, she comes home
and tells me my fortune.
It will be a good year for me.
Luck. Happiness. Surprises.

But how can it ever be a good year
thousands of miles away from home?

SPRING

I pass the cobbler every day,
sitting on the sidewalk,
working on shoes.

Every day, I stop and watch him
cutting the leather in smooth curves,
pulling the needle, tugging the thread tight.
"I learned how when I was ten,"
he says. "My family, they needed the money."
He nods. "You're a lucky boy.
Come here, go to school."

But I don't want to go to school,
where the English words
taste like metal in my mouth.
I'd rather stay here,
watching his fingers craft shoes
the way a sculptor carves shapes out of stone.

Long ago, you had to be rich
to have your own music
caught in a cage.

But now, almost anyone
can own a bird
in a fancy bamboo house.
And even if you can't,
you can still come here and listen,
to this bird shop
in the middle of Chinatown,
where it sounds
like the woods in spring.

When we left Hong Kong,
we had to pack quick.
So many things got left behind—
a country
a language
a grandmother
and my animal chess game.

But tonight my father comes home
and hands me a package.
"I found it in a bookshop," he says. "Surprise!"
Inside, the red and green pieces sleep close together.
But on the board, the cat pounces on the mouse,
the mouse terrifies the elephant.
And I beat my sister.

Just like home.

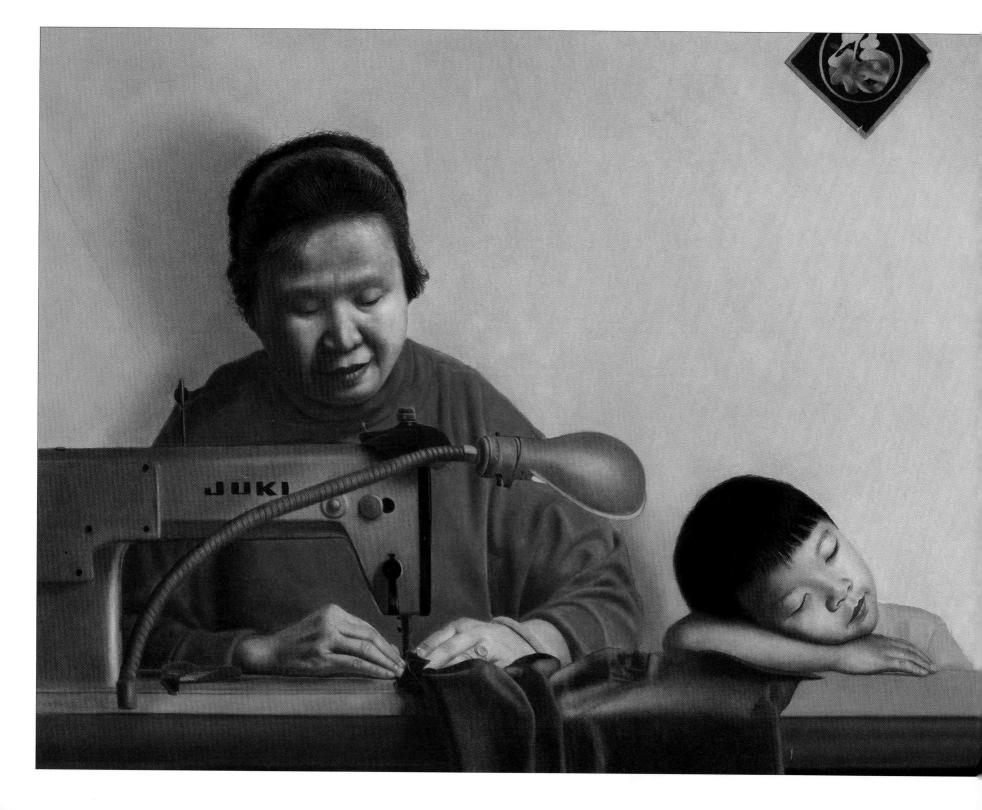

Twelve hours every day
the needle on her sewing machine
gobbles up fabric,
turning miles of cloth
into pants and jackets, skirts and dresses.
After supper I sit beside my mother,
listening to the hum of the motor,
the soft chatter
of the hungry needle.

Sometimes I fall asleep beside her,
the sound of her work
a lullaby.

It's a long, dark, rattling subway ride
to the lake in Queens
where, once a year,
there are dragons.
Carved heads and painted tails,
the dragons race across the water,
the rowers straining,
the drums pounding,
the watchers cheering
and making bets.
One day I'll be a part of it,
rowing to the drumbeat,
instead of standing on dry land,
shouting my throat sore,
wishing my favorite boat to victory.

Everyone's windows are open,
but no breeze comes.
The laundry sags on the clothesline.
I can smell hot oil, chicken sizzling.
I can hear mah-jongg tiles slap the table,
neighbors talking
in Chinese and English.
Nai-wen leans out her window.
"Let's go outside," she calls.
"Meet you on Eldridge Street."
I wave back at her.

Maybe we'll find enough kids
to play kick-the-can,
my favorite American game.

FALL

In the fish tank,
the carp are crowded
nose to tail, scale to scale.
In plastic tubs on the sidewalk,
eels slither, frogs scramble.

My mother points out the fish she wants.
He waves his tail gently
and looks straight at me.

That night I say I'm sick
so I won't have to eat him.

I've been waiting
weeks and weeks
for the Moon Festival to come.
Moons are everywhere,
stacked high on the counters of every store,
round and perfect, sweet as clouds,
with a golden egg yolk in the center.

But every day Papa still says,
"Not yet."

Until tonight!
Up the stairs, out on the roof,
and Papa lights the lantern.
I can see paper fires
on every roof,
tiny moons glowing.
Our apartment house is drifting loose,
floating free in the night sky.

My favorite shop is dark inside,
warm and quiet.
Near the ceiling,
dragons, birds, butterflies
soar on paper wings.
Masks watch me from the walls.
On the shelves are
bowls and chopsticks,
paper finger traps,
bamboo snakes.
Like things I remember from home,
except there
they weren't for sale.

No matter how often I come,
or how long I stay,
no one ever asks me
to buy a thing.

If you have money in your pocket,
you're never hungry
in Chinatown.
Curried squid, crispy cakes,
tofu in syrup, fried noodles,
sweet buns with coconut
or bean paste in the middle.
Mama will say I spoiled my dinner,
but I don't care.
I'm first in line for fish balls,
bobbing in brown soup, in a white carton,
salty as the ocean,
steaming hot,
ten for a dollar,
delicious.

WINTER
AGAIN

The arcade—lights flash, bells ring,
boys shout, jump, run.
Quarters in my pocket—which game?
Through a smudgy window,
I see a chicken who'll play tic-tac-toe.
We pick X's and O's.
The chicken goes first.
She beats me,
and a handful of grain
showers down for her to eat.
I feed the slot every quarter I have
just to watch her
gobble up her winnings.

New Year's Day!
Noodles for breakfast,
sweet rice cakes.
A red envelope stuffed with money
in my pocket.
And lions in the street outside.
I fly downstairs to be there
when they come—
leaping, pouncing,
prancing, roaring,
jumping, dancing,
shaking their neon manes.
Drums beat
feet stamp
hands clap
voices shout
Chinatown,
this is Chinatown!

For my mother and father

T 67544

My Chinatown: *One Year in Poems*
Copyright © 2002 by Kam Mak
Printed in the U.S.A. All rights reserved.
www.harperchildrens.com
Library of Congress Cataloging-in-Publication Data
Mak, Kam.
 My Chinatown / one year in poems by Kam Mak.
  p.   cm.
 Summary: A boy adjusts to city life away from his home in Hong Kong, in the
Chinatown of his new American city.
 ISBN 0-06-029190-7 — ISBN 0-06-029191-5 (lib. bdg.)
 [1. Chinatown (New York, N.Y.)—Fiction.   2. Emigration and immigration—
Fiction.   3. Chinese Americans—Fiction.   4. New York (N.Y.)—Fiction.]   I. Title.
PZ7.M2817 My   2002   2001016686
[E]—dc21   CIP
                                                              AC

Typography by Al Cetta
1   2   3   4   5   6   7   8   9   10
❖
First Edition